The Wind in the Willows

Look for all the
SCHOLASTIC JUNIOR CLASSICS

SCHOLASTIC JUNIOR CLASSICS

The Wind
in the
Willows

Retold from
Kenneth Grahame
by Ellen Miles

Illustrations by
Steven Smallman

SCHOLASTIC INC.

New York   Toronto   London   Auckland   Sydney
Mexico City   New Delhi   Hong Kong   Buenos Aires

Copyright © 2002 by Ellen Miles.

Based on *The Wind in the Willows* by Kenneth Grahame, which was first published in 1908. All rights reserved. Published by Scholastic Inc. SCHOLASTIC and associated logos are trademarks and/or registered trademarks of Scholastic Inc.

ISBN 0-439-22456-X

24 23 22 21 20   19 20 21 22

Printed in the U.S.A.   40

First Scholastic printing, March 2002

Contents

The Wind in the Willows

The Riverbank

Chapter One

MOLE had been working very hard all morning, spring cleaning his little underground home. He was tired and his back hurt, and now something was calling him from up above. Spring was moving in the air, and suddenly Mole could not stand to be inside for one more minute. He threw down his broom. It was time to get outside. He scraped and scratched and scrabbled and scrooged, digging busily with his little paws and muttering to himself, "Up we go! Up we go!" until at last, pop! he came out into the sunlight, and he was rolling in the warm grass of a big meadow.

"This is wonderful!" he said. "This is

better than cleaning!" Mole felt sunshine and soft breezes. He heard the birds singing. He jumped up and ran joyfully all the way across the meadow, to the hedge that ran along the far side.

Spring was bursting out everywhere. Everyone else in the meadow was very busy, but Mole thought that made it even more fun to be free.

Then he came to the edge of a river. Mole had never seen a river before. It glinted and gleamed and sparkled as it ran, full of bubbles and swirls and motion. Right away, Mole loved it. He trotted along the side of the river until he was tired. As he rested on the grassy shore, he noticed a dark hole in the opposite bank. He thought dreamily about what a nice snug home it would make. Then he saw a face.

A little brown face, with whiskers, small neat ears, and thick silky hair.

It was the water rat!

"Hello, Mole!" said Rat. "Would you like to come over?"

"Oh, yes! But — how?" asked Mole.

Rat bent over and unfastened a rope. Then he stepped into a little blue-and-white boat. It was just the perfect size for two animals. Rat rowed across the river and helped Mole into the boat.

"What a wonderful day!" said Mole as Rat started rowing again. "Do you know I've never been in a boat before, in my whole life?"

Rat was shocked.

"It's nice," said Mole as he leaned back in his seat and felt the boat sway lightly under him.

"*Nice?* It's the *only* thing," said Rat as he rowed. "Believe me, my young friend, there is nothing better than simply messing about in boats. Simply messing," he went on dreamily, "messing — about — in — boats. Messing —"

"Look out, Rat!" cried Mole suddenly.

It was too late. The boat ran right into the bank. Dreamy Rat lay on his back in the bottom of the boat, his heels in the air.

"— about in boats," Rat went on, picking himself up with a laugh. "I'll show you! Why don't we spend the day on the river?"

Mole waggled his toes and gave a happy sigh. "What a day I'm having!" he said. "Let's start right away!"

"Hold on a minute!" said Rat. He tied up the boat, climbed into his hole, and came back out, carrying a big picnic basket.

"What's inside?" asked Mole, wriggling with curiosity.

"There's cold chicken," replied Rat, "coldhamcoldbeefpicklesrollscheesesand-wicheslemonadesoda —"

"Oh, stop, stop," cried Mole. "This is too much!"

"Do you really think so?" asked Rat. "The other animals are always telling me I don't bring enough!" He set the picnic basket in the center of the boat and began to row again.

Mole was so happy. He leaned back and let his paw trail in the sparkling, rippling water. Rat just rowed on, letting him dream. "So you really live on the river?" Mole asked finally. "What a wonderful life."

"By it and with it and on it and in it," said Rat. "It's brother and sister to me, and company, and food and drink, and washing. It's my world, and I don't want any other. Winter or summer, spring or autumn, it's always fun and exciting."

"But isn't it lonely sometimes?" Mole asked. "Just you and the river, and no one else to talk to?"

"No one else to —" Rat smiled. "You're new. You don't know. The riverbank is so crowded nowadays! Otters, kingfishers, ducks, everybody busy and happy."

"What's over *there*?" asked Mole, waving a paw toward a dark forest on one side of the river.

"That's the Wild Wood," said Rat. "We don't go there very much, we river-bankers."

"What are the animals like there?" asked Mole, a little nervously.

"W-e-ll," replied Rat, "let me see. The squirrels are all right. And the rabbits — some of 'em, anyway. And then there's Badger, of course. He lives right in the heart of it. Nobody bothers *him*. They'd better not."

"Who would bother him?" asked Mole.

"Well, there are weasels and foxes and so on," said Rat. "I'm friends with some of them. But you can't really trust them, and that's a fact."

"And what's past the Wild Wood?" Mole asked.

"Past the Wild Wood is the Wide World," said Rat. "I've never been there,

and I'm never going
ther. Now then! Here's ou

Rat turned the boat into a qu
with green, grassy banks. It was so beau
ful that Mole could only gasp, "Oh, my!"

Rat tied up the boat, helped Mole step
out, and lifted the picnic basket onto the
shore. Mole wanted to unpack it all by
himself, and Rat was happy to let him. He
lay on the grass and rested while his excited friend spread out the tablecloth and
took everything out of the basket. "Oh,
my!" Mole said when he saw all the food.

When their picnic was ready, Rat said,
"Help yourself, old fellow!" Mole was glad
to. He was very hungry.

"What are you looking at?" asked Rat,
after they'd been eating for a while.

"I am looking," said Mole, "at a streak of
bubbles moving along the water."

"Bubbles? Aha!" said Rat. He made a
little noise.

A wide shiny nose showed itself above

the edge of the bank, and Otter hauled himself out of the river and shook the water from his coat.

Rat introduced Mole to Otter.

"Nice to meet you," said Otter. "Such a day!" he went on. "Everyone is out on the river today. I came up here to try to get a moment's peace."

There was a rustle from the hedge behind them, and a stripy head peeked out.

"Come on, old Badger!" shouted Rat.

Badger trotted forward a step or two, then grunted, "Hmph! Company." He turned his back and disappeared.

"We won't see any more of *him* today," said Rat. "Well, tell us, Otter, who's out on the river?"

"Toad's out," replied the Otter, "in his brand-new boat. New clothes, new everything!"

The two animals looked at each other and laughed.

"Once it was nothing but sailing," said

Rat. "Then he got bored with that. Last year it was houseboating. Now it's rowing."

Just then Toad rowed by, splashing as he worked his oars. Rat called and waved, but Toad was concentrating too hard on his rowing to answer back.

The three animals talked for a little longer. Then Otter dove back into the river and disappeared, leaving a streak of bubbles on the water.

Soon it was time to go. The afternoon sun was getting low as Rat rowed gently homeward. Mole was getting restless. "Ratty! Please, *I* want to row now!" he said suddenly.

Rat shook his head with a smile. "Wait until you've had a few lessons. It's not as easy as it looks."

Mole was quiet for a minute or two, but he began to feel more and more jealous of Rat, rowing so easily along. He knew he could do it just as well. He jumped up and grabbed the oars, knocking Rat out of the way.

Mole tried to row but completely missed the water. His legs flew over his head, and he found himself lying on top of Rat in the bottom of the boat. He grabbed at the side of the boat, and the next moment — *sploosh*!

Over went the boat!

Oh, my, how cold the water was, and oh, how *very* wet it felt as Mole sank and rose and sank again. Then a paw grabbed him by the back of his neck. It was Rat, and he was laughing.

Rat helped Mole to shore, hauled him out, and set him down on the bank to dry out. Then Rat dove into the water again to save the boat and the picnic basket.

Finally, they got back into the boat. "Ratty," said Mole, "I am so sorry. Will you forgive me?" He felt so embarrassed and ashamed of himself.

"Of course!" said Rat. "Listen, why

don't you come and stay with me for a while? My house isn't fancy like Toad's, but it's very comfortable. I'll teach you to row and swim."

Mole couldn't believe his ears — or his luck. He was so happy he couldn't even speak. But Rat understood.

When they got home, Rat lit a fire. Then he told Mole river stories till suppertime. Mole listened with all his might. After supper, Rat took a very sleepy Mole upstairs to the best bedroom. Mole fell asleep to the sound of the river lapping near his window, and the wind in the willows above.

The Open Road

Chapter Two

"RATTY," said Mole one bright summer morning, "may I ask you a favor?"

Rat was sitting on the riverbank, singing a little song he'd composed about his friends the ducks. He was very proud of it. It began, "All along the backwater, through the rushes tall, ducks are a-dabbling, up tails all!"

When Rat was making up songs it could be hard to get his attention. Mole tried again. "Will you take me to meet Mr. Toad?"

"Why, certainly," said Rat, jumping to his feet. "Get the boat out, and we'll paddle up there right now. Toad will be happy to see us!"

"He must be a very nice animal," said Mole as he got into the boat and took the oars. He had learned to row very well by then.

"Toad is the best of animals," replied Rat. "He can be boastful, but he's a good animal, that Toady."

Rounding a bend in the river, they saw a handsome old redbrick house, with green lawns rolling down to the water's edge. "That's Toad Hall," said Rat, "and that's his boathouse, where we'll leave the boat. The stables are over there. Toad is very rich, you know." Mole rowed into the boathouse. None of the boats there seemed used. Rat looked around. "I see," he said. "Toad must be tired of boating. I wonder what's next? Let's go find him. I'm sure we'll hear all about it."

Rat and Mole found Toad sitting outside, looking at a large map that was spread out on his lap.

"Hooray!" he cried, jumping up. "I was

just going to send a boat down the river for you, Ratty. Come inside and have something to eat!"

"Let's just sit for a minute, Toady!" said Rat, throwing himself into a chair. Mole sat down, too, and told Toad what a nice house he had.

"Finest house on the whole river," cried Toad. "Or anywhere else, for that matter," he could not help adding.

Rat nudged Mole. Toad saw him do it, and turned very red. Then he burst out laughing. "I'm sorry, Ratty," he said. "I can't help boasting. And it's not a bad house, is it? Now, look. You've got to help me!"

"It's about your rowing, I suppose," said Rat. "You still splash a lot, but with practice and some coaching —"

"Oh, pooh! Boating!" interrupted Toad. "Silly, boyish fun. I gave that up *long* ago. Waste of time. Come with me, and I'll tell you about my wonderful new plan!"

He led them to the stable yard and showed them his shiny new Gypsy wagon. It was canary yellow, with green trim and red wheels.

"This is the life!" cried Toad. "A cart like this, and the open road! Here today, off to somewhere else tomorrow! Travel, change, interest, excitement! And this is the finest cart ever built. Come inside and look." Mole followed Toad inside the cart. Rat snorted, stuck his hands into his pockets, and stayed where he was. Inside there were sleeping bunks, a little table that folded up against the wall, a stove, book-shelves, and even a birdcage with a bird in it.

Toad proudly showed everything off. "We'll have everything we need when we start out on our adventures this afternoon," he told Mole as they walked back outside.

"I beg your pardon," said Rat slowly,

"but did I hear you say something about *we* and *start* and *this afternoon*?"

"Now, dear Ratty," said Toad, "you *have* to come. I can't manage without you, so don't argue. You can't stick to your boring old river all your life. I want to show you the world!"

"I don't care," said Rat. "I'm not coming, and that's that. And I *am* going to stick to my boring old river. And Mole's going to stick with me, aren't you, Mole?"

"Of course I am," said Mole loyally. "I'll always stick with you, Rat. Still, it sounds as if a journey might have been fun!"

Rat felt bad. He wanted Mole to be happy.

Toad was watching both of them closely. "Come in and have some lunch," he said, "and we'll talk it over. We don't have to decide right away."

During lunch, Toad ignored Rat and

tried to persuade Mole. He talked about how wonderful life would be on the open road until Mole was so excited he could hardly sit still. Rat couldn't stand to disappoint his friends, so by the end of lunch it was decided. They were going.

After lunch, they hitched up the horse and set off. It was a golden afternoon. Birds called to them cheerily, and the rabbits they passed held up their paws and said, "Oh, my!"

Later, tired and happy and miles from home, they stopped and ate supper, sitting on the grass by the side of the cart. Toad talked big about all his plans, while the stars came out and a yellow moon rose to keep them company. At last they climbed into their little bunks in the cart. "Well, good night!" Toad said. "This is the life! Talk about your old river!"

"I don't talk about my river," said Rat. "I *think* about it," he added quietly. "I think about it all the time!"

Mole reached out from under his blanket, felt for Rat's paw in the darkness, and gave it a squeeze. "I'll do whatever you like, Ratty," he whispered. "Should we run away tomorrow morning and go back to our dear old hole on the river?"

"No, no, we'll see it out," whispered Rat. "It wouldn't be safe to leave Toad alone. It won't be long. His fads never last."

The end was even nearer than Rat suspected.

Toad slept very late the next morning, so Mole and Rat took care of the horse, and lit a fire, and washed last night's dishes, and got things ready for breakfast. They were tired by the time Toad woke up, all fresh and happy and full of talk about what an easy, simple life they were living.

Later, they were strolling along the road when they heard a hum. Glancing back, they saw a small cloud of dust coming toward them — fast! — and they heard a

distant *beep-beep*! They paid no attention, until suddenly there was a blast of wind and a whirl of sound that made them jump for the nearest ditch! The *beep-beep* was loud now, as a magnificent motorcar thundered by in a cloud of dust.

The old gray horse reared up in fear, and Toad's beautiful cart went into the ditch.

Rat was furious. "You villains!" he shouted at the motorcar, shaking both fists, "you — you — road hogs! I'll report you!"

Toad sat down in the middle of the dusty road and stared in the direction of the disappearing motorcar. *"Beep-beep,"* he said softly, a happy smile on his face.

"*Beep-beep!* What a sight!" he murmured. "Poetry in motion! The *only* way to travel! Oh, bliss! Oh, *beep-beep*! Oh, my!"

"Oh, *stop*, Toad!" cried Mole.

"And to think I never knew!" Toad went on. "All those wasted years . . . Now that I know, oh, how I'll speed along, flinging carts into the ditch as I go by! Stupid little canary-colored carts!"

"What are we going to do with him?" asked Mole.

"Nothing," replied Rat firmly. "He has a new craze. Ignore him."

Rat and Mole began walking to town. When Toad caught up to them, Rat told him he would have to go to the police station and file a complaint, then get the cart fixed. "Mole and I will find an inn, and we'll stay there until the cart is ready," he said.

"Police station! Complaint!" cried Toad. "Me *complain* of that beautiful vision? Fix the cart? I'm done with carts forever."

Rat turned to Mole. "You see?" he said. "I give up. When we get to town we'll take a train back to the riverbank."

They got Toad back to Toad Hall and into bed. Then Mole rowed their boat home, and he and Rat had a late supper in their cozy riverside home.

The next day Mole was sitting on the bank fishing when Rat came strolling along. "Heard the news?" he said. "Everybody's talking about it. Toad went up to town and ordered a large and very expensive motorcar."

The Wild Wood

Chapter Three

MOLE had been wanting to meet Badger, but Rat kept putting it off. "He'll turn up when he wants to," he told Mole.

"Couldn't you ask him here for dinner?" said Mole.

"He wouldn't come," replied Rat. "Badger hates society and invitations and dinner and all that."

"Well, then, what if we go visit *him*?" suggested Mole.

"Oh, he wouldn't like that at *all*," said Rat. "He's very shy. Besides, it's out of the question, because he lives in the very middle of the Wild Wood. You just wait. He'll come along someday."

But Badger never came along, and

when summer ended and cold and frost kept them indoors, Mole started to think about Badger again. Mole was restless, because Rat's winter routine was not so exciting.

In winter, Rat slept a lot. During the day he scribbled poetry or did household chores, and there were always animals dropping in to visit and talk about their wonderful memories of the summer. They talked of flowers and sun and boating and swimming and all the other adventures they'd had.

All of that was nice, but Mole was a little bored. So one afternoon he decided to go out alone and explore the Wild Wood — and maybe meet Badger.

It was a cold afternoon when he slipped out of the warm parlor where Rat was dozing. Everything looked different outside, with bare ground and no leaves on the trees, but Mole liked the way it looked.

He wasn't scared at all when he first en-

tered the Wild Wood. Twigs crackled under his feet and logs tripped him, but that was all fun and exciting. He went on, deeper into the Wood, where it was darker and the trees crouched nearer and nearer. Then everything became very still. It got darker very quickly as the sun went down.

Suddenly, Mole began to feel a little afraid. He saw scary faces peeping out at him, and he heard strange whistling and pattering sounds all around him. He kept moving, trying not to be frightened, even when a rabbit ran by him and whispered, "Get out of here while you can, you fool!" He kept going until he was too scared and too tired to go any farther, and then he curled up in a nest of dry leaves and tried to sleep, wishing he had listened to Rat.

Meanwhile, Rat dozed in his parlor until the fire crackled and woke him up. He looked around for Mole to ask him if he knew a good rhyme for something or other.

But Mole was not there.

The house seemed very quiet, and Mole didn't answer when Rat called for him. He went into the hall and saw that Mole's cap was missing from its peg and his boots were gone.

Rat left the house, hoping to find Mole's tracks. There they were, sure enough, running straight into the Wild Wood. Rat set right out, following the tracks.

It was already getting dark when he reached the first trees. He went straight into the Wood, looking for any sign of his friend. He saw the scary little faces and heard the frightening noises, but he ignored them, calling "Moly, Moly, Moly! Where are you? It's me! It's old Rat!"

He had hunted through the Wood for an hour or more when at last to his joy he heard a little answering cry. He made his way through the darkness to the foot of an old beech tree. "Ratty! Is that really you?"

came a voice from inside a little hole in the tree.

Rat crept into the hole, and there was Mole, exhausted and shaky. "Oh, Rat!" he cried, "I've been so frightened!"

"Oh, I know," said Rat soothingly. "You shouldn't have come here alone, Mole. I tried to tell you."

Mole started to feel better, knowing that Rat was there.

"Now, then," said Rat, "we really should start for home while there's still a little light left. It's too cold to spend the night here." He went to look out of the hole. "Oh, dear," he said.

"What's up, Ratty?" asked Mole.

"Snow is up," replied Rat, "or rather, *down*. It's snowing hard."

Mole looked outside. The Wild Wood looked completely different, covered in a carpet of white.

"Well, well," said Rat. "We still have to

get home. The problem is, I don't exactly know where we are. And this snow makes everything look so different."

They set out bravely, trying to convince themselves that they were going the right way.

An hour or two later they sat down on a stump to catch their breath and decide what to do. They were tired and wet and bruised from falling. The snow was getting so deep that they could hardly drag their little legs through it, and the trees were thicker than ever. There seemed to be no end to the Wild Wood, and no beginning, and no way out.

"We can't sit here very long," said Rat. "It's too cold and the snow is getting deeper." He looked around. "Look here, where the ground is all hilly and humpy. We'll find some sort of shelter, a cave or a hole with a dry floor, out of the snow and wind. We can rest there and then try again."

So they got up and looked around one

of the hilly areas. Suddenly, Mole tripped and fell.

"Oh, my leg!" he cried. He sat up on the snow, holding his leg in both his front paws.

"Poor old Mole!" said Rat. "Let's see." He bent down to look. "You've cut your shin, sure enough. I'll bandage it with my handkerchief."

"I must have tripped over a hidden branch or a stump," said Mole miserably.

"It's a very clean cut," said Rat, looking at it closely as he bandaged it. "That wasn't done by a branch or a stump. It looks as if it was made by a sharp edge of something metal. Funny!" He thought for a while and looked around.

"Who cares what did it?" Mole said. "It hurts just the same."

But Rat was busy scraping in the snow. He scratched and shoveled and explored, all four legs working busily. "Hooray!" he cried suddenly.

"What have you found, Ratty?" asked Mole.

"Come and see!" said Rat, dancing a happy little jig.

Mole took a good look. "Well," he said, "it's a boot scraper! So? Why dance around a boot scraper?"

"But don't you see what it *means*?" cried Rat impatiently.

"Of course I see what it means," replied Mole. "It means that some very careless person left his boot scraper lying in the middle of the Wild Wood, just where it's sure to trip everybody. Very thoughtless."

"Oh, Mole!" cried Rat. "Come and dig!" And he started working again, making the snow fly.

Finally, he uncovered a very shabby doormat.

"There, what did I tell you?" exclaimed Rat.

"Absolutely nothing whatever," replied Mole. "So you've found another piece of junk. Do your little dance, and then let's go."

"Are you saying," cried Rat, "that this doormat doesn't *tell* you anything?"

"Really, Rat," said Mole, "let's be serious. Who ever heard of a doormat *telling* anyone anything?"

Rat couldn't believe how silly Mole was being. "Quiet down and dig," he said. "It's our last chance if we want to sleep where it's dry and warm."

Rat dug like mad, and Mole helped, even though he thought Rat was being ridiculous.

Ten minutes later, Rat called Mole over. "Look!" he said.

In the side of what had seemed to be a snowbank was a little door, painted dark green. There was a doorbell and a little brass plate that said MR. BADGER.

Mole was so surprised and happy that he fell backward into the snow. "Rat!" he cried. "You're amazing! You figured it out!

You knew that a boot scraper meant there would be a doormat and that a doormat meant there would be a door! Oh, if only I had your brains!"

"Since you don't," interrupted Rat, "you're probably going to sit in the snow all night and *talk*. Get up and ring that doorbell, while I knock!"

Rat banged on the door and Mole pushed the doorbell. Deep inside, they heard a bell ring.

Mr. Badger

Chapter Four

THEY waited patiently for what seemed like a very long time. Finally, the door opened just enough to show a long nose and a pair of sleepy, blinking eyes.

"Who is disturbing me on such a night? Speak up!" said a gruff and suspicious voice.

"Oh, Badger," cried Rat, "let us in, please. It's me, Rat, and my friend Mole, and we've lost our way in the snow."

"Why, Ratty!" exclaimed Badger in a very different voice. "Come in, both of you. Well, I never! Lost in the snow! And in the Wild Wood, too, at this time of night! Come in!"

Badger wore a bathrobe and slippers,

and he was carrying a candlestick in his paw. He had probably been on his way to bed when they knocked. He patted both their heads. "This is not the sort of night for small animals to be out," he said. "Come into the kitchen. There's a fire there."

Badger shuffled on in front of Rat and Mole, carrying the light. They followed him down a long, gloomy passage until they found themselves in a large, warm kitchen.

There was a redbrick floor and a big fireplace with two high-backed benches on either side. In the middle of the room was a long table, with benches to sit on and an armchair at one end. There were rows of plates on the shelves, and from the rafters overhead hung hams, bundles of dried herbs, onions, and baskets of eggs. It was a cozy, welcoming place.

Badger sat them down on a bench to warm themselves at the fire and told them to take off their wet coats and boots. Then he brought them bathrobes and slippers, and he cleaned Mole's cut with warm water and bandaged it nicely. Soon Mole and Rat were so warm and content that the Wild Wood felt miles and miles away.

When they were completely warm Badger told them it was time for supper. He had brought out all kinds of delicious food, and they ate and ate, telling Badger the whole story of how they had come to his door. Badger sat in his armchair and listened and never once said, "I told you so." Mole began to feel very friendly toward him.

After supper, the three of them sat around the fire again and talked some more. "Now, then!" Badger said. "What's the news from your part of the world? How's old Toad?"

"Oh, from bad to worse," said Rat. "Another bad smashup last week. He's a terrible driver."

"How many has he had?" asked Badger gloomily.

"Smashes or machines?" asked Rat. "Oh, well, after all, it's the same thing with Toad. This is the seventh."

"He's been in the hospital three times," put in Mole.

"Badger!" said Rat. "We're his friends. Shouldn't we do something?"

Badger thought hard. "Of course, you know I can't do anything *now*," he said finally.

His friends understood. No animal is expected to do anything difficult during winter. Everybody knows winter is a time for resting.

"But when spring comes," continued Badger, "we'll teach him a lesson. We'll — you're asleep, Rat!"

"Not me!" said Rat, waking up with a jerk.

"He's been asleep two or three times since supper," said Mole, laughing. He himself was feeling wide awake, though he didn't know why. The reason, of course, was that he had grown up living underground like Badger, so he felt at home in Badger's house. Rat was used to the breezy river, and being underground made him feel sleepy.

"Well, it's time for bed," said Badger. "Come along, you two, and I'll show you your room."

He took them to a long room that was half bedroom and half barn. Badger's win-

ter supplies took up half the room: piles of apples, turnips, and potatoes, baskets full of nuts, and jars of honey. There were also two little white beds that looked soft and inviting. Mole and Rat jumped right in and fell asleep.

They slept late, and when they came down to breakfast the next morning they found two young hedgehogs sitting on a bench at the table, eating oatmeal out of wooden bowls. The hedgehogs dropped their spoons, rose to their feet, and ducked their heads respectfully when Mole and Rat came in.

"Sit down, sit down," said Rat pleasantly, "and finish your oatmeal. Where did you come from? Did you lose your way in the snow?"

"Yes, sir," said the older of the two hedgehogs. "Me and little Billy here, we was trying to find our way to school and of course we lost ourselves, sir, and Billy got frightened. And at last we found Mr. Badger's back door, and decided to knock, sir, for Mr. Badger is a kindhearted gentleman, as everyone knows —"

"I understand," said Rat. He and Mole began to help themselves to bacon and eggs. "And what's the weather like outside? You don't have to 'sir' me quite so much," he added.

"Oh, very bad, sir, the snow is very deep," said the hedgehog. "You won't get out today."

"Where's Mr. Badger?" asked Mole.

"He's in his study, sir," replied the hedgehog, "and he said he was going to be very busy this morning, and he shouldn't be disturbed."

Everybody knew what *that* meant. Badger was taking a nap.

The doorbell rang, and Rat sent Billy, the smaller hedgehog, to see who it was. There was some stamping in the hall, and then Billy came back with Otter, who threw his arms around Rat.

"Thought I might find you here," said Otter cheerfully. "They were all worried about you along the riverbank this morning. But I knew that when people were in trouble they usually went to Badger, so I came straight here, through the Wild Wood and the snow! It was beautiful, coming through the snow as the red sun was rising against the black tree trunks! I could have played in the snow all morning!"

"Weren't you at all nervous?" asked Mole.

"Nervous?" Otter showed a gleaming set of strong white teeth as he laughed. "Not me. Now, how about some breakfast? I'm starving."

Otter had just finished one plate full of eggs and bacon and was about to have some more when Badger came in, yawning and rubbing his eyes. "It must be almost lunchtime," he said to Otter. "Better stay and eat with us. You must be hungry this cold morning."

"Oh, yes!" replied Otter, winking at Mole. "The sight of these greedy young hedgehogs stuffing themselves makes me feel positively famished."

The hedgehogs, who were just beginning to feel hungry again after their oatmeal, looked timidly up at Mr. Badger but were too shy to say anything.

"Here, you two youngsters be off home to your mother," said Badger kindly.

The rest of them sat down to lunch together. Mole found himself next to Mr. Badger, and since the other two were talking about river news, he decided to tell Badger how at home he felt. "Once you're underground," Mole said, "you know exactly where you are. Nothing can happen to you. You're the boss. And when you want to, up you go."

Badger smiled. "That's exactly what I say," he replied. "There's no real peace or happiness, except underground. And if you want to expand — why, a dig and a scrape, and there you are! If you decide your house is too big, you stop up a hole or two, and there you are again! And there's no *weather*. Look at Rat. A couple of feet of floodwater, and he has to move. Take Toad. Toad Hall is the best house in these parts. But what if a fire breaks out — where's Toad? No, up and outside is good for some things, but underground — that's my idea of *home*."

Mole agreed, and Badger got very friendly with him. "When lunch is over," he said, "I'll take you all around this little place of mine. I can see you'll appreciate it."

After lunch, when the other two had settled themselves near the fire for a long talk on the subject of eels, Badger lit a lantern and told Mole to follow him. He gave him a complete tour of the main tunnels. Mole was very impressed.

When they got back to the kitchen they found Rat pacing restlessly. Being underground was getting on his nerves, and he was eager to get back to his river. He already had his overcoat on. "Come on, Mole," he said as soon as he saw them. "We have to leave while it's daylight. Don't want to spend another night in the Wild Wood."

"It'll be all right," said Otter. "I'm coming along with you, and I know every path with my eyes closed. I'll take care of you."

"You don't have to worry, Ratty," added Badger. "My passages run farther than you think, including some secret ones. You can leave by one of my shortcuts."

Rat was ready to go, so Badger led the way along a damp tunnel that twisted and turned for what seemed like miles. At last they saw daylight ahead. Badger said a quick good-bye and pushed them through the opening. Then he rearranged the vines and leaves that covered his secret hole and turned back.

Rat and Mole and Otter found themselves standing on the very edge of the Wild Wood. In front of them was a wide open field, and far off they could see the river shining in the last light of day. Otter led them across the snowy field. Mole glanced back once at the Wild Wood, and seeing its dark shadows made him even more sure that he was happy to live where he did, in the fields and meadows that weren't quite so wild. He was happy to have met Badger, and he would always remember his adventure in the Wild Wood, but right then he could hardly wait to get back to Rat's cozy house.

Home Sweet Home

Chapter Five

MOLE and Rat were on their way home late one December afternoon, after a long day of exploring with Otter. It was a chilly, gray day, and they were looking forward to being home. Rat was walking a little ahead as Mole trotted along behind him, thinking about supper. It was dark by then, and he was very hungry. Suddenly, Mole felt a certain tingle and smelled a familiar smell. He stopped dead in his tracks, trying to figure out what it was. Then it came to him. Home! His very own home, the one he'd left on that spring-cleaning day so many months ago. They must be passing near it. Oh, his happy home! He knew it wasn't anything fancy, but suddenly he wanted to see it.

"Ratty!" he called, full of excitement, "Come back!!"

"Oh, come on, Mole!" replied Rat, still plodding along.

"*Please* stop, Ratty!" begged poor Mole. "You don't understand! It's my home, my

old home! I just smelled it, and it's close by here, really close. And I *have* to go to it. I have to! Oh, Ratty! Please, please come back!"

But Rat was very far ahead by then, too far to hear what Mole was saying. He smelled snow in the air, and he wanted to hurry home. "Mole, we can't stop now!" he called back. "We'll come for it tomorrow, whatever it is." He kept going, without waiting for an answer.

Poor Mole stood alone in the road, feeling torn in two directions. He was a loyal friend and did not want Rat to go on alone. But, oh, how his home was calling to him. Finally, he pushed himself forward, following Rat. It nearly broke his heart, but he did it.

He caught up to Rat, who began chatting cheerfully about how they'd build a fire and have a lovely supper when they got home. Finally, he noticed how upset

Mole was. "Mole," he said, "you seem tired. Let's sit down here on these tree stumps for a minute and rest. We're almost home."

Mole sank down onto a tree stump and tried to keep from crying, but it was no use. He gave up. He cried and cried, sobbing his heart out.

Rat felt terrible. He let Mole cry for a while, and then he said gently, "What is it, old fellow? What's the matter?"

Poor Mole could hardly talk, he was crying so hard. "I know it's a sh-shabby, dingy little place," he sobbed, "not like your cozy rooms or T-Toad's beautiful hall or Badger's great house, b-but it was my own little home and I loved it, and I-I went away and forgot all about it and then I smelled it, and I called and you wouldn't listen, Rat, and you wouldn't turn back, and I had to leave it, and I thought my heart would break. We c-could have just gone and had one look at it, Ratty, just one look, but you wouldn't turn back, Ratty! Oh, dear, oh, dear!"

Thinking about it made him start sobbing all over again, and he began to cry even harder.

Rat patted Mole gently on the shoulder. He waited until Mole's crying calmed down and he was just sniffling. Then he got up and said, "Well, now we really should be going, old chap!" He set off, going back the way they'd come.

"Where are you g-going, Ratty?" cried Mole.

"We're going to find that home of yours, old fellow," replied Rat, "so come along. We'll need your nose to find it."

Now *Mole* felt bad, and he tried to protest, but Rat wouldn't listen. Cheerfully, he led Mole along, back to the spot where Mole had first stopped. "Now," he said, "use your nose!" He stepped back and watched until, suddenly, Mole stood very still for a moment, then stuck his twitching nose into the air. He ran forward a few steps, then back, then forward again. Rat followed closely as Mole, looking like a sleepwalker, crossed a ditch, scrambled through a hedge, and nosed his way across an open field.

Suddenly, without any warning, he dived. But Rat was watching, and he followed him right down the tunnel. Soon they were standing at Mole's little front door, with a sign that said MOLE END over the doorbell. Mole took a lantern from a nail on the wall and lit it. Then Rat could see a neat little garden, with benches and tables and statues and even a little fishpond.

Mole looked happily at all his things. Then he led Rat inside and lit a lamp. When he saw how dusty and shabby everything looked, he threw himself into a chair, upset again. "Oh, Ratty!" he cried. "Why did I bring you to this cold little place on a night like this, when you could have been home by now!"

Rat ignored him. He ran here and there, opening doors, inspecting rooms and closets, and lighting lamps and candles. "What a perfect little house this is!" he called out cheerily. "Everything here, and everything in its place! We need a good fire. I'll take care of that. You try to clean things up a bit. Let's go, old chap!"

Mole jumped up and dusted and polished, and Rat soon had a cheerful blaze roaring in the fireplace. He called to Mole to come and warm himself, but Mole had another fit of the blues. He plopped down on a couch. "Rat," he moaned, "what about supper, you poor, cold, hungry, tired animal? I have nothing to give you — not a crumb!"

"Oh, come on," Rat said. "Don't give up so easily. Let's go see what we can find. I'm sure there's something here."

They hunted through all the cupboards

and drawers and found a can of sardines, some crackers, and a sausage. "There we are!" said Rat.

"No bread!" groaned Mole. "No butter, no —"

"No steak, no ice cream!" continued Rat, grinning. "Let's be happy for what we *do* have. Plenty to eat, and such a nice little house to eat it in. Why don't you tell me all about it while we set the table. Where did you get that nice old painting, for example?"

Once Mole began to talk about his house, he couldn't stop. While Rat set the table Mole told him all about how he'd built the house and went on with the story of how he'd gotten every piece of furniture and every lamp. Rat nodded and smiled, getting hungrier and hungrier. Finally, they were ready to sit down to eat — but just then there was a scuffling noise from outside!

Next, Mole and Rat heard voices. "Now,

all in a line, hold the lantern up a bit, Tommy! Where's young Bill? We're all waiting —"

"What's up?" asked Rat.

"I think it must be the field mice," said Mole. "They go around singing carols at this time of year. They always come to Mole End last. I used to give them hot drinks, and even supper sometimes. It will be like old times to hear them again."

"Let's see them!" cried Rat. He ran to open the door.

There in the entryway were eight or ten little field mice standing in a group, red scarves around their necks. As the door opened, one of the older ones said, "Now, then, one, two, three!" and their shrill little voices rose on the air, singing an old Christmas carol.

"Well sung, boys!" cried Rat when they were done. "And now come in and warm yourselves by the fire and have something hot!"

"Yes, come in, field mice," cried Mole. "This is like old times! Shut the door after you. Pull up that bench to the fire. Now, you just wait a minute, while we — oh, Ratty!" he cried. "What are we doing? We don't have a thing to give them!"

"You leave that to me," said Rat. He turned to the field mice and called out, "You, with the lantern! I want to talk to you. Tell me, are there any shops open this late?"

"Why, certainly, sir," replied the field mouse.

"Then listen!" said Rat. "I want you to go right out and get —" His voice dropped, and Mole couldn't hear much after that. Rat gave the mouse some money and a big basket and sent him on his way.

The rest of the field mice sat in a row by the fire, too shy to talk much until Mole asked about their younger brothers and sisters. That got them going. Meanwhile, Rat made some hot chocolate and passed it around.

Before long, the first mouse came back with a very full basket of food. In a few minutes supper was ready and they sat down, with Mole at the head of the table. Everyone talked and laughed and ate until they were full.

After dinner, the mice headed home, carrying leftovers for their younger brothers and sisters. Mole and Rat sat by the

fire and talked about their day, until Rat,
with a tremendous yawn, said, "Mole, old
chap, I'm ready for bed."

He climbed into his bunk and tucked
himself in and fell asleep right away.

Mole got into bed, too, but before he
closed his eyes he looked around at the

room and all his familiar things. He knew now that as much as he loved his adventurous new life, he still loved home, too. It was good to think that he always had this place to come back to.

Mr. Toad

Chapter Six

ONE day in spring, Badger arrived at Rat's door, looking very serious. "The hour has come!" he said.

"What hour?" asked Rat.

"*Whose* hour is more like it," replied Badger. "It's Toad's hour! The hour of Toad! I said I would deal with him as soon as winter was over, and I'm going to deal with him today!"

"Hooray!" cried Mole. "I remember now! We'll teach him to be a sensible Toad!"

"This very morning," continued Badger, "another new and very powerful motorcar will arrive at Toad Hall. We must go up there and rescue Toad right away."

They set off up the road, Badger leading the way, and reached Toad Hall to find a huge, shiny new motorcar, painted bright red (Toad's favorite color), standing in front of the house. Mr. Toad, wearing goggles, a cap, and an enormous overcoat,

came swaggering down the steps, pulling on his gloves.

"Hello!" he cried cheerfully. "You're just in time to come with me for a —" He stopped when he noticed how serious his friends looked.

Badger walked up the steps. "Take him inside," he said sternly. Mole and Rat pulled Toad up the stairs.

"Now then!" Badger said to Toad, when the four of them stood together in the Hall. "First of all, take those ridiculous things off!"

"I won't!" replied Toad. "What is the meaning of this?"

"Take them off him, then, you two," ordered Badger.

They had to lay Toad on the floor, kicking and calling them names, to get his driving clothes off. When they stood him up again, he was calmer.

"You knew it had to come to this, sooner or later, Toad," Badger said. "You've ignored all our warnings, you've gone on spending all your money, and you're giving us animals a bad name with your reckless driving and your smashes and your fights with the police. We animals never allow our friends to make fools of themselves beyond a certain limit, and you've reached that limit. Come with me into the living room and we'll have a talk. We'll see whether you come out of that room the same Toad that you went in."

He took Toad firmly by the arm, led him into the living room, and closed the door behind them.

"That's no good!" said Rat. "*Talking* to Toad'll never cure him. He'll *say* anything."

He and Mole made themselves comfortable in armchairs and waited patiently. Through the closed door they could hear Badger's voice, rising and falling. Soon they heard Toad crying.

After a while the door opened, and

Badger came back in, leading Toad by the paw. Toad looked guilty and sad.

"Sit down, Toad," said Badger kindly, pointing to a chair. "My friends," he went on, "I am happy to tell you that Toad has at last seen the error of his ways. He is truly sorry for his behavior, and he has promised to give up motorcars forever."

"That is very good news," said Mole.

"Very good news, indeed," agreed Rat. "If only —"

He was looking very hard at Toad as he said this and could not help thinking he saw a twinkle in his eye.

"There's only one thing more to be done," continued Badger. "Toad, I want you to repeat, before your friends here, what you told me in the living room. First, you are sorry for what you've done, and you see how silly it was."

There was a long, long pause. Toad looked around wildly while the others waited. "No!" he said finally. "I'm *not* sorry. And it wasn't silly at all! It was wonderful!"

"What?" cried Badger. "Didn't you just tell me, in there —"

"Oh, yes, yes, in *there*," said Toad impatiently. "I'd have said anything in *there*. You were so convincing, Badger. But I've been thinking about it, and now I know I'm not sorry at all, so I really shouldn't say I am."

"Then you don't promise," said Badger, "never to touch a motorcar again?"

"Certainly not!" replied Toad. "In fact, I faithfully promise that the very first motorcar I see, *beep-beep*! Off I'll go in it!"

"Told you so, didn't I?" Rat said to Mole.

"Very well, then," said Badger, rising to his feet. "Since you won't change your mind, we'll have to try something else. You've often asked us three to come and stay with you in this handsome house of yours. Well, now we're going to. We'll stay until you see things our way. Take him upstairs, you two, and lock him up in his bedroom."

"It's for your own good, Toady, you know," said Rat kindly, as Toad, kicking and struggling, was hauled up the stairs by his two faithful friends. "Think what fun we'll all have together, once you get over this."

"We'll take care of everything for you till you're well, Toad," said Mole.

"No more fights with the police, Toad," said Rat as they pushed him into his bedroom.

"And no more weeks in the hospital," added Mole, turning the key on him.

They went downstairs, Toad shouting at them through the keyhole, and sat down with Badger to decide what to do next.

"It's going to take a while," said Badger, sighing. "I've never seen Toad so stubborn. But we'll wait until he gets it out of his system. Meanwhile, we'll have to take turns watching him."

So the three friends took turns sleeping in Toad's room at night, and they divided the day up between them. At first Toad was impossible. He would set up the bedroom chairs in the shape of a motorcar and sit there making car noises until he "crashed," somersaulting to the floor and knocking the chairs over. As time passed, he did this less and less, but he also seemed to get quieter and sadder.

One morning it was Rat's turn on duty. He took over from Badger, who was ready for a long walk. "Toad's still in bed," he told Rat outside the door. "He says he wants to be left alone and not to worry about him. Now, you look out, Rat! When Toad's quiet like this, there's sure to be something up. I know him."

Badger left for his walk, and Rat opened the door.

"How are you today, old chap?" asked Rat cheerfully as he approached Toad's bed.

At first there was no answer. Finally, a feeble voice replied, "Thank you for asking, dear Ratty! But first, tell me how you and Mole are."

"Oh, we're all right," replied Rat. "Mole is going out for a walk with Badger. They'll be out till lunchtime, so you and I will spend the morning together. Now, jump up. Don't lie there moping on a fine morning like this!"

"Dear, kind Rat," said Toad, "if you only knew how far I am from 'jumping up'! But don't worry about me. I hate being a burden to my friends, and I don't think I'll be one much longer." Then, in a weak little voice, Toad tried to convince Rat that he was so sick he needed Rat to fetch a doctor from town. "By the way," he added, "I hate to bother you, but could you also call my lawyer? I think it might be time to make a will."

That really scared Rat. He hurried out of the room, not forgetting to lock the door carefully. He didn't know what he should do. He wished he could talk to Mole and Badger, but they weren't there.

"It's best to be on the safe side," he said to himself. "Toad has been pretty sick before, but I've never heard him ask for a lawyer! If there's nothing really the matter, the doctor will tell him so." So he ran off to the village to find the doctor.

Toad, who had hopped out of bed as soon as he heard the key turn in the lock, watched from the window until Rat disappeared down the driveway. Then, laughing, he dressed as quickly as possible in his nicest suit, filled his pockets with cash, knotted the sheets from his bed together, tied one end to the window frame, and scrambled out. He slid lightly to the ground and went off in the opposite direction, whistling a merry tune.

It was a gloomy lunch for Rat when Badger and Mole came back and he had to tell them what had happened. They weren't very nice about it, to tell the truth. But Badger pointed out that what was done was done and that talking about it wouldn't help. "Toad got away," he said, "and the worst part of it is that now he thinks he's so smart he can get away with anything. Who knows what he'll do next? I think we should stay here for a while so we can pick up the pieces."

Little did Badger know how long it would be before Toad came home.

Meanwhile, Toad was walking happily along the highway, very pleased with himself for the way he'd tricked Rat. He walked along thinking about how smart he was until he reached a little town, where he saw a restaurant. He went in, ordered some lunch, and sat down to eat.

He was about halfway through his meal

when he heard a familiar sound, out on the street. *Beep-beep!* It came nearer and nearer until the car came to a stop near the restaurant. Toad was very excited. Then the people in the motorcar came into the restaurant, talking about the wonderful drive they'd had in their wonderful car that wonderful morning. Toad listened until he couldn't stand it anymore. He slipped out of the room, paid his bill, and went outside to see the car. "It can't hurt just to *look* at it," he told himself.

The car was parked nearby, without anyone around. Toad walked around it, taking a good look.

"I wonder," he said to himself, "I wonder if this sort of car *starts* easily?"

Before he knew what he had done, Toad had jumped into the car and started it up. He stepped on the gas and drove down the street, faster and faster, forgetting everything else. He got onto the highway and drove even faster. He was Toad again, Toad at his best, Toad the Terror.

And, before the day was over, he was Toad in jail, sentenced to twenty years behind bars.

Toad's Adventures

Chapter Seven

TOAD was in jail, all alone in a dark, damp cell in the middle of a large castle-like building with many gates and guards. He had plenty of time to think about what a mess he'd made of things. How smart and kind his friends had been! How thoughtless he had been! He *deserved* to be in jail.

He refused to eat, and spent all his time crying and telling himself what a bad Toad he was.

Now, the warden had a daughter who helped her father at the jail. She loved animals, and she felt sorry for Toad. She begged her father to let her take care of him. The warden was tired of Toad's sulk-

ing and crying, so he was glad to say yes. Later that day, the warden's daughter brought Toad his dinner.

"Now, cheer up, Toad," she said. "Dry your eyes and be a sensible animal. Try to eat some dinner. See what I've brought?"

Toad lay on the floor, kicking and crying. But the stew she had brought him smelled very good. Maybe life wasn't all bad. He had his friends, and maybe they would be able to help. The world was a wonderful place, and with luck he could be free to enjoy it again someday. After all, he was Toad! Smart, wonderful Toad. Everything would work out.

Toad sat up and dried his eyes. He began to eat, and he began to talk about himself, and his house, and how important he was, and how great his friends thought he was.

The warden's daughter saw how happy it made him to boast. "Tell me about Toad Hall," she said. "It sounds beautiful."

So he told her about the boathouse, and the fishpond, and the garden, and about the dining hall, and the fun the other animals had there when they were gathered around the table and Toad was at his best, singing songs and telling stories. Then she wanted to know about his animal friends, and he told her all about them and how they lived. By the time she said good night, Toad was himself again. He sang a little song or two, then fell asleep and had all kinds of happy dreams.

Toad and the warden's daughter became friends after that. She felt sorry for him. Of course, *he* thought she was in love with him.

One morning she said, "Toad, listen. I have an aunt who is a washerwoman."

"There, there," said Toad graciously. "That's all right. Nothing to be ashamed of."

"Oh, be quiet, Toad," said the girl. "My aunt does the washing for all the prisoners here. She takes out the washing on Monday morning and brings it back on Friday evening. This is a Thursday. Now, this is what I think. You're very rich, and she's very poor. I think you could make a deal with her. She could lend you her dress and bonnet, and you could escape from the castle as the official washerwoman. You do look alike."

Toad was insulted. "But Mr. Toad of Toad Hall can't go around disguised as a washerwoman!"

"Then you can stay here as a toad," she replied.

Toad knew when he was wrong. "You are a good, kind, smart girl," he said, "and I am a stupid toad. I would love to meet your aunt."

The next night the warden's daughter brought her aunt to Toad's cell. He gave her some money, and she gave him a dress, an apron, a shawl, and an old black bonnet.

"Now it's your turn, Toad," said the girl. "Take off that coat of yours. You're fat enough as it is." Shaking with laughter, she helped Toad put on the clothes, then sent him on his way.

The disguise worked perfectly, and

Toad was out of jail before he knew it. Still dressed in the washerwoman's clothes, he walked toward town. He headed straight for the train station to buy a ticket for a train home. That was when he realized he had left all his money in the pocket of his coat, back at the jail!

He tried to convince the ticket seller that he could pay later, after he'd been home, but it was no use. Toad watched the train get ready to leave without him, feeling terrible. How could this have happened? Now he would probably be caught again, and thrown back into jail.

As he walked along next to the train, he came to the engine. The engineer was standing nearby.

"Hello, there!" said the engineer. "What's the matter? You don't look happy."

"Oh, sir!" said Toad, starting to cry. "I am a poor unhappy washerwoman, and I lost all my money, and I can't pay for a ticket, and I have to get home tonight somehow. What am I going to do?"

"That's too bad," said the engineer. "Lost your money, and can't get home. You probably have some kids waiting for you, too."

"Lots of them!" sobbed Toad. "And they'll be hungry, and playing with matches, and fighting —"

"Well, I'll tell you what I'll do," said the engineer. "You say you're a washerwoman. Well, I'm an engineer, and it's dirty work. My wife gets awfully tired of washing all my clothes. If you'll wash a few shirts for me when you get home, I'll give you a ride on my engine."

Toad scrambled up into the cab of the engine, happy again. Of course, he had never washed a shirt in his life and didn't know how, but he thought he could send the engineer some money instead. That would be just as good.

Soon the train moved out of the station. As they picked up speed Toad watched fields and trees and hedges and cows and horses fly by, and he knew every minute was bringing him nearer to Toad Hall, and good friends, and money, and a soft bed to sleep in, and good things to eat, and the chance to tell everyone how smart he had been. He began to skip up and down and sing, which surprised the engineer.

Then Toad noticed that the engineer had a puzzled expression on his face. He was leaning over the side of the engine and listening hard. Then he stuck his head out the window to look back. "It's very strange," he said. "We're the last train tonight, but I could swear that I hear another train following us!"

Toad stopped skipping. He stopped singing. He didn't even want to *think* about who might be on that other train.

The engineer kept watching. "Yes, it is

another train!" he said. "I think it's chasing us."

Toad groaned.

"They're catching up!" cried the engineer. "And it's full of policemen, all calling 'Stop, stop, stop'!"

Toad fell to his knees and begged, "Save me, save me, dear, kind Mr. Engineer. I am not a simple washerwoman! I have no children waiting for me! I am a toad, the well-known Mr. Toad. I have just escaped from a terrible dungeon. If they catch me, I'll be locked up again!"

The engineer looked at him very sternly and said, "Now, tell the truth. What were you put in prison for?"

"Nothing much," said Toad, blushing. "I just borrowed a motorcar while the owners were at lunch. I didn't mean to steal it."

The engineer looked very serious and said, "You have been a very bad toad, and

I should turn you in. But you're in trouble and I won't desert you. I don't like motor-cars, for one thing, and I don't like being ordered about by policemen, for another. And the sight of an animal in tears always makes me feel softhearted. So cheer up, Toad! I'll do my best. We might beat them yet!"

He pushed the train to top speed, but the other train was still catching up. Finally, he turned to Toad and told him that his best chance was to jump off the train just after it came out of the next tunnel.

As soon as they came out of the tunnel Toad jumped, rolled down a short bank, picked himself up, scrambled into the woods, and hid. Then out of the tunnel burst the other engine, roaring and whistling, the policemen shouting, "Stop! stop! stop!" When they were past, Toad had a good laugh for the first time since he was thrown into jail.

But he soon stopped laughing when he
realized that it was now very late and dark
and cold, and he was in an unknown forest, with no money and no chance of supper, and still far from friends and home.
He was afraid to leave the shelter of the

trees, so he headed into the woods, even though they seemed dark and scary.

Toad was tired and angry and hungry, too. Finally, he crawled inside a hollow tree, made himself a bed from branches and dead leaves, and fell asleep.

Wayfarers All

Chapter Eight

MEANWHILE, Rat was restless, and he did not exactly know why. Summer was almost over, and the birds were beginning to fly south. Even though Rat loved his life on the river, he began to wonder. What would it be like to see those far-off places?

Rat wandered through the familiar fields. How would it be to leave them behind? Feeling a little sad, he went back to the river. At least his dear old river never packed up and went away.

Rat spotted a bird, a swallow to be exact, in the reeds. Soon it was joined by another, and then by a third. Rat knew they were about to fly south. "What, *already*?"

he asked, strolling up to them. "What's the hurry?"

"Oh, we're not flying off yet, if that's what you mean," replied the first swallow. "We're only making plans. Talking over what route we're taking this year, and where we'll stop, and so on. That's half the fun!"

"Couldn't you stay for just this year?" suggested Rat wistfully. "You have no idea what good times we have here, while you are far away."

"I tried staying one year," said another swallow. "For a few weeks it was fine, but when it got dark and cold, I couldn't stand it. Finally, I headed south, alone. It was snowing hard when I left, and it was hard flying, but I'll never forget the feeling of the hot sun on my back as I finally flew down to the warm lakes that lay so blue below me. No, I learned my lesson. I'll never do that again."

"Ah, yes, the call of the south!" twittered the other two dreamily. "Oh, do you remember —" and forgetting Rat, they talked happily about their other home. Rat listened, and for the first time he was really tempted to go. He closed his eyes and thought about sun and warmth, and when he opened them again the river seemed cold and gray. Then he shook himself.

"Why do you ever come *back*?" he asked the swallows.

"We love it here, too," said the first swallow. "We get homesick, and we want to return to the fields and meadows and barns."

They started talking again, but Rat walked away, toward a nearby hill. He climbed up to look out over his familiar view. Was there something else out there, somewhere else that he might love even more?

Then he heard footsteps. It was another rat, a very dusty one. The wayfarer said hello and sat down. He was thin, and his face was wrinkled. He wore small gold earrings, a blue sweater, and a pair of old, patched pants. He carried his things tied up in a blue cotton handkerchief.

"I like the smell of clover, and the sight of cows in the meadow," he said, after

he'd rested for a moment. "It's quiet here, very peaceful. You have a good life, here by the river."

"Yes, it is *the* life, the only life to live," answered Rat dreamily. He didn't sound quite as sure as he usually did.

"That may be so," said the stranger, "but still, I'm on my way south. I'm a seafaring rat. I have been all over this world."

Rat asked the stranger to tell him about his travels, and the sea rat talked for a long time, spinning tales of distant lands, beautiful, exotic cities, and the delicious food and drink of other countries.

"That reminds me," said Rat, "you must be hungry. Will you have lunch with me? My hole is nearby."

"That's kind of you," said the sea rat. "I *am* hungry. But do you think you could bring it out here? I'll fall asleep if I go inside, but if we stay outside I can tell you more stories."

"What a good idea," said Rat, and he

hurried home to pack up his picnic basket with bread and sausage and other things he thought the sea rat would like.

When he came back, they unpacked the food and ate and ate. When they weren't quite so hungry anymore, the sea rat began to talk again, telling the story of how he'd found his way from sunny Spain all the way to this hill up north.

Rat loved every detail of the story. Sea Rat went on and on about his travels and adventures, and Rat began to feel as if he were dreaming a beautiful, exciting dream. Finally, Sea Rat stood up. "And now," he said, looking into Rat's eyes, "I must start off again, on to the warm south for more adventure. And you will follow me, won't you? Adventure is calling you. Listen, and come!"

His voice died away, and Rat sat staring as Sea Rat disappeared down the road.

Without thinking, Rat got up and carefully packed the picnic basket. Without thinking, he went home, gathered together a few belongings, and put them in a knapsack. Like a sleepwalker, he threw the knapsack over his shoulder, chose a walking stick, and stepped outside just as Mole appeared at the door.

"Where are you off to, Ratty?" asked Mole, surprised.

"Going south, with the rest of them,"

murmured Rat in a dreamy voice. "Adventure is calling me!"

He tried to walk past Mole, but Mole wouldn't let him. He saw something in Rat's eyes, something that frightened him. Rat was not himself. It was as if he had been hypnotized. Mole pulled Rat back inside.

Rat struggled for a few moments, and then he gave in. Mole helped him to a chair, where he sat, looking shaky and exhausted. Then Rat began to cry. Mole closed the door, threw Rat's knapsack into a closet, and sat down quietly near his friend, waiting for the tears to stop. Finally, Rat fell asleep, and Mole let him nap.

When Rat woke up, he seemed more like himself again. Mole sat down and tried to cheer him up. "What happened?" he asked.

Ratty tried to explain things, but it was

hard. How could he explain the magic of Sea Rat's tales? The spell was broken now, and he could hardly believe how strong it had been.

Mole could see that Rat still seemed sad. He even seemed to have lost interest in his beloved river. Mole began to talk about how nice it was with fall coming, how the farmers were harvesting their crops, how the apples were ripening on the trees, and how everyone was looking forward to another snug winter in their cozy homes.

Soon Rat sat up and joined in. His eyes were a little brighter, and he seemed interested in his old life again.

Mole slipped away for a moment and came back with a pencil and some paper. "It's been quite a while since you wrote any poetry," he said. He knew Rat would feel much better if he wrote a few lines.

Rat pushed the paper away at first. But

Mole left the room, and when he peeked in a little later, Rat was scribbling away. Then Mole knew for sure that Rat would be all right. His dreams of going south would stay dreams, while he stayed home on the river, where he was truly happiest.

The Further Adventures of Toad

Chapter Nine

TOAD woke up cold and stiff, and for a moment he wasn't sure where he was. Then he remembered. He was free! He crawled out of the hollow tree where he'd spent the night and headed down the road, hoping to find someone who could give him directions home.

After a while, he realized that there was a canal running next to the road, a man-made stream used for transportation. Soon he saw a horse plodding along the tow path, pulling a rope attached to a barge that floated on the canal.

Steering the barge was a stout woman wearing a sunbonnet.

"A nice morning, ma'am!" she said to Toad.

"It is, ma'am!" responded Toad politely as he walked along the tow path next to her. "At least, it's a nice morning for people who aren't in trouble, like I am. I'm off to see my married daughter, who sent for me. I don't know what's wrong, but I fear the worst. Meanwhile, I had to leave my washing work behind, and my children. And now I've lost all my money, and I don't know where I am!"

"Where does your married daughter live, ma'am?" asked the bargewoman.

"She lives near the river, ma'am," replied Toad, "close to a fine house called Toad Hall."

"Toad Hall? Why, I'm going that way myself," replied the bargewoman. "You come along in the barge with me, and I'll give you a lift."

She steered the barge close to the bank,

and Toad jumped in. *Toad's luck again!* he thought. *I always come out on top!*

"So you're in the washing business, ma'am?" asked the bargewoman politely as they glided along.

"That's right," said Toad.

"And do you enjoy washing?" asked the bargewoman.

"I love it," said Toad. "I'm never so happy as when I have both arms in the washtub."

"What good luck, meeting you!" said the bargewoman.

"What do you mean?" asked Toad nervously.

"Well," replied the bargewoman, "I like washing, too, but I have trouble keeping up with it, especially when my husband goes off hunting, the way he did today, and leaves me to take care of the boat."

"Oh, well," said Toad, "the washing will keep. Forget it. And maybe your husband will catch something good for dinner."

"I just can't forget it," said the barge-woman. "But you'll be happy to know that there's a heap of dirty clothes in the corner of the cabin. You can have your fun washing them, and it'll be a real help to me. There's a tub, and soap, and a bucket to haul up water from the canal. Then I'll know you're enjoying yourself instead of just sitting here, bored."

"Why don't you let me steer?" said Toad. "Then you can do the washing your own way."

"Let you steer?" replied the barge-woman, laughing. "It takes some practice to steer a barge right. Besides, it's boring work, and I want you to be happy. No, you do the washing, and I'll stick to steering."

Toad was cornered. He thought about trying to jump off the barge, but it was too far from the bank. *Oh, well,* he thought, *I suppose any fool can* wash!

He got the tub and the soap and the dirty clothes and started in. But Toad could not figure out how to get the clothes clean. He splished and splashed and kept losing the soap in the sudsy water. His back was aching, and his paws were getting all crinkly.

Finally, the bargewoman began to laugh. She laughed so hard she could hardly talk. "I've been watching you all the time," she gasped. "Some washer-woman you are!"

Toad lost his temper.

"You — you — bargewoman!" he shouted. "Don't you dare talk to me like that! Washerwoman, indeed! I am a toad, a very well-known, respected, distinguished toad! And I will not be laughed at by a bargewoman!"

The woman moved nearer to him and looked under his bonnet. "Why, so you are!" she cried. "Well, I never! A nasty, crawly toad on my nice, clean barge! Now, that is a thing that I will *not* have."

She grabbed Toad by one front leg and one back leg and threw him off the barge. He landed in the cold water with a splash and swam for shore, which wasn't easy with his washerwoman's dress tangling around his legs. The bargewoman was still laughing as he climbed up the bank, and Toad felt angrier than ever. He ran after the barge, which had moved down the canal, until he caught up with the horse that was towing it. He unfastened the rope, jumped on the horse, and galloped off.

"Stop! Stop!" cried the bargewoman as her barge ran into the bank and stopped moving.

"I've heard that song before," said Toad, laughing as he rode off.

The horse was old and tired and it could not gallop for long. Soon it was walking slowly along, but Toad didn't care. He wasn't angry anymore, just impressed with how smart he had been to get revenge in such a clever way.

After a while, the horse stopped to eat, and Toad looked up to see an old Gypsy wagon. There was a man sitting beside it, cooking a delicious-smelling stew in an iron pot over an open fire. When Toad smelled the food he was suddenly hungrier than ever.

The Gypsy and Toad looked at each

other. Then the Gypsy spoke. "Want to sell that horse of yours?"

Toad was surprised, but he saw right away that selling the horse might be a very good idea. "What?" he said. "Sell this beautiful young horse of mine? Oh, no, it's out of the question. Who's going to take the washing home to my customers every week? Besides, I love him, and he loves me. Anyway, he's a very fine horse, and you probably couldn't afford him." Toad paused. "How much were you going to offer?"

The Gypsy looked the horse over, and then he looked Toad over. "Nickel a leg," he said.

"A nickel a leg?" cried Toad. "Now, let me just add that up."

He climbed off the horse, sat down by the Gypsy, and counted on his fingers. At last he said, "A nickel a leg? That comes to exactly four nickels! Oh, no, I couldn't

think of taking four nickels for this beautiful young horse of mine."

"Well," said the Gypsy, "I'll tell you
what I'll do. I'll make it five nickels, but
that's my last word."

Toad sat and thought. He was hungry
and had no money and he was still far
from home. In some ways, five nickels
seemed like a lot. On the other hand, it
did not seem like much to get for a horse.
But then again, the horse hadn't cost him
anything, so whatever he got was a profit.
At last he said firmly, "Look here, Gypsy!
I'll tell you what we will do, and this is *my*
last word. You give me five nickels and as
much breakfast as I can eat, and I'll give
you my horse."

The Gypsy grumbled but finally agreed.
He gave Toad the money. Then he filled
up a plate with the delicious stew, and
Toad ate and ate until he couldn't eat any
more.

By the time Toad said good-bye to the

Gypsy and the horse, he felt much better. His stomach was full, his clothes were dry, and he had money in his pocket. As he walked along, he thought of his adventures and escapes, and how, when things seemed at their worst, he had always managed to find a way out. He began to swell with pride. "Ho, ho!" he said to himself as he marched along with his chin in the air. "What a clever Toad I am! My enemies shut me up in prison, I walk out. They chase me with engines and policemen, I escape. I am thrown into a canal by a nasty fat woman. So what? I swim ashore, I steal her horse, and sell it for a whole pocketful of money and an excellent breakfast! Ho, ho! I am Toad, the handsome, the popular, the successful Toad!" He got so puffed up that he made up a song all about himself and sang it loudly as he walked. But Toad's pride was about to have a great fall.

As he was walking along the highway, he heard something familiar. *Beep-beep!* A motorcar! Toad was excited. *I'll flag them down,* he thought, *and they'll give me a ride. With luck, maybe I'll end up driving to Toad Hall in a motorcar! That will show Badger!*

He stepped right out into the road to stop the motorcar, but when it slowed down he suddenly became very pale. His knees started shaking, and he fell over onto the road in a heap. The car was the very one he had stolen from the restaurant! "Oh, what a stupid Toad I have been! Now I'll end up back in jail!" he moaned.

The motorcar came closer and stopped. Two men got out and looked at Toad, and one of them said, "Oh, dear! This is very sad! Here is a poor old washerwoman who has fainted in the road! Let's lift her into the car and take her to the village."

Carefully, they lifted Toad into the motorcar and propped him up with soft cushions. Then they headed off again.

Toad's courage came back as soon as he

knew that his disguise had fooled them. He opened his eyes.

"Look!" said one of the men, "she's better already. The fresh air is doing her good. How do you feel now, ma'am?"

"Thank you kindly, sir," said Toad in a feeble voice. "I'm feeling much better!"

"Good," said the man. "Now keep still, and don't try to talk."

"I won't," said Toad. "I was just thinking that if I could sit in the front seat, beside the driver, I could get more fresh air in my face, and I would feel even better."

"What a smart woman!" said the man. "Of course you shall." So they helped Toad into the front seat.

Toad was almost himself again by now. He sat up, looked around, and tried to resist the old temptations he was feeling. But then, of course, he gave in. He turned to the driver.

"Please, sir," he said, "I wish you would let me try to drive the car for a little. I've been watching you carefully, and it looks so easy and so interesting, and I would like to be able to tell my friends that I once drove a motorcar!"

The driver laughed. "Bravo, ma'am! I like your spirit. Have a try."

Toad scrambled into the driver's seat, took the steering wheel in his hands, pretended to listen to the instructions the man gave, and started driving. He went very slowly and carefully at first.

The men applauded, and Toad heard them saying, "Imagine a washerwoman driving a car so well the first time!"

Toad went a little faster, then a lot faster.

He heard the men call out, "Be careful, washerwoman!"

But soon Toad was going full speed. The rush of air in his face and the hum of the engine made him almost lose his mind with happiness. "Washerwoman, ha!" he shouted recklessly. "Ho, ho! I am Toad, the motorcar snatcher, the prison breaker — Toad, who always escapes! Now you'll know what driving really is, for you are in the hands of the famous, the skillful, the fearless Toad!"

"This is the Toad who stole our car!" one of the men shouted. "Grab him! We'll take him back to the police station!" They should have remembered to stop the motorcar somehow before doing something like that. The car crashed through a hedge and into a muddy little pond.

Toad picked himself up and ran off as fast as he could, scrambling through hedges, jumping ditches, pounding across fields, till he was breathless and tired and had to slow down. When he got his breath back and started to think about what had happened, he began to giggle. Then he began to laugh, and he laughed till he had to sit down under a hedge. "Ho, ho!" he cried. "Toad again! Toad, as usual, comes out on top! Clever Toad, great Toad, *good* Toad!"

Then he burst into song again, until suddenly he saw two large policemen running toward him!

Toad started running again. "Oh, my!" he gasped. "What an idiot I am! Singing songs again!"

He looked back and saw that the policemen were catching up to him. He ran and ran, but they kept getting closer. He was running so fast that he didn't see the river until he had fallen into it and was swept away!

He bobbed along, trying to grab the reeds along the bank, but the current was too strong. "Oh, my!" gasped poor Toad, "I'll never steal a motorcar again! I'll never sing another boastful song!" Finally, he saw a big dark hole in the bank, just above his head, and he reached up with a paw and grabbed the edge and held on.

Then a twinkle appeared from deep in the dark hole. As it came closer, Toad saw that it was a face. A familiar face!

A little brown face, with whiskers, small neat ears, and thick silky hair.

It was Rat!

Toad Learns the Worst

Chapter Ten

RAT grabbed Toad and hauled him out of the river.

"Oh, Ratty!" Toad cried. "I've been through so much since I saw you last! I got

through it all with courage and intelligence. Just wait until you hear —"

"Toad," said Rat, "you go upstairs right now and take off that old cotton rag that looks as if it once belonged to some washerwoman, and wash yourself, and put on some of my clothes. Now, stop swaggering and arguing, and go!"

When Toad had changed, he joined Rat for lunch. While they ate, Toad told Rat all his adventures, making himself sound like a hero and making all the worst parts sound fun and exciting.

When he was finally finished, Rat was quiet for a moment. Then he said, "Now, Toady, I don't want to make you feel bad, but seriously, don't you see what an idiot you've been making of yourself? You're telling me you have been handcuffed, imprisoned, starved, chased, terrified out of your life, insulted, and thrown into the water! Where's the fun in that? And all because you had to go steal a motorcar. You know you've never had anything but trouble from motorcars from the moment you first saw one. It's one thing to drive them. Fine. But why do you have to *steal* them?"

When Rat had finished, Toad sighed and said, "You're right, Ratty! How smart you always are! Yes, I've been an idiot, I can see that. But now I'm going to be a good toad. We'll have a quiet chat, and then I'm going to walk down to Toad Hall and settle back in. I've had enough of adventures. I just want to live a quiet life at home."

"Walk down to Toad Hall?" cried Rat. "What are you talking about? Are you telling me you haven't *heard*?"

"Heard what?" said Toad, turning pale.

"Are you telling me," shouted Rat, "that you haven't heard about the stoats and weasels?"

"What, the Wild Wooders?" cried Toad, trembling.

"And how they've taken over Toad Hall?" continued Rat.

Toad began to cry.

"When you — were away," Rat said, trying to be polite about Toad being in jail, "well, everyone was talking about it, not only along the river, but even in the Wild Wood. The Wild Wood animals said it served you right and that you would never come back again, never, never!"

Toad just nodded.

"But Mole and Badger," Rat went on, "they kept saying that you would come back again soon. They didn't know exactly how, but somehow!"

Toad began to sit up in his chair and smile a little.

"So they moved their things to Toad Hall," Rat told him, "and planned to stay there and have it all ready for you when you came back. They didn't guess what was going to happen, but they were suspicious. Now I come to the worst part of my story. One dark night, when it was raining cats and dogs, a band of weasels, armed to the teeth, crept up to the front entrance of Toad Hall. At the same time, some ferrets got into the backyard and offices, and some stoats took over the greenhouse."

Toad looked shocked.

But there was more. Rat went on. "Mole and Badger were sitting by the fire in the living room when those bloodthirsty villains broke down the doors and rushed in upon them from every side. Badger and Mole fought as hard as they could, but what was the use? They were taken by surprise, and what can two animals do against hundreds? The stoats and weasels and ferrets beat them up and threw them out into the cold and rain, and the Wild Wooders have been living in Toad Hall ever since," finished Rat. "They lie in bed half the day, and make a mess, and eat your food, and make bad jokes about you.

And they're telling everybody that they've come to stay for good."

"Oh, have they!" said Toad getting up. "I'll see about that!" He marched down the road, talking angrily to himself, until he got near his front gate. But there was a ferret guarding the gate, and he would not let Toad pass. He went back and told Rat.

"What did I tell you?" said Rat. "It's no good. They have guards everywhere. You'll just have to wait."

But Toad was not ready to give up. He got out the boat and rowed up the river to Toad Hall. When he saw his old home, he slowed down to look around. Everything seemed quiet. The house looked the same as always, as if it were waiting for him to come back. Quietly, he paddled closer. He was just passing under the bridge, when . . . *CRASH*!

A huge stone, dropped from above, smashed through the bottom of the boat. The boat sank, and Toad splashed around

in the deep water. Looking up, he saw two stoats leaning over the bridge, laughing at him. Toad swam to shore and went back to tell Rat what had happened.

"Well, what did I tell you?" asked Rat. "And now look what you've done! Ruined my boat *and* that nice suit of clothes I lent you! Really, Toad!"

Toad knew he'd been bad. He apologized to Rat for losing his boat and spoiling his clothes. And he promised to listen to Rat and not do anything else until Rat told him to.

"All right," said Rat, "sit down and have some supper. Mole and Badger will be here soon, and we'll talk about what to do."

"Oh, yes, Mole and Badger," said Toad. "I almost forgot about them. What happened to them?"

"Nice of you to ask!" said Rat. "While you were riding around the country in expensive motorcars, those two poor animals have been camping out, watching over your house, keeping an eye on the stoats and the weasels, and planning how to get your property back for you. You don't deserve to have such true and loyal friends, Toad. Someday, when it's too late, you'll be sorry you didn't appreciate them while you had them!"

"I'm an ungrateful Toad, I know," sobbed Toad. "Let me go out and find them. I'll go out into the cold, dark night, and — hold on! Didn't I just hear the clink of dishes on a tray? Supper's here! Come on, Ratty!"

Rat remembered that poor Toad had been eating prison food for a long time, so he followed him to the table.

They had just finished their meal when there was a heavy knock at the door. When Rat opened it, in walked Mr. Badger.

He looked as if he hadn't been home in a long time. His shoes were muddy and his clothes were wrinkled. He came up to Toad, shook his paw, and said, "Welcome home, Toad! Oh, what am I saying? Home, ha! This is a terrible homecoming. Poor Toad!" Then he sat down to eat.

Soon there was another knock. This time it was Mole, who also looked very shabby. "Hooray! Here's old Toad!" cried Mole, beaming. "We never dreamed you would turn up so soon! You must have escaped, you smart toad!"

Rat grabbed Mole's elbow, but it was too late. Toad was already puffing up with pride.

"Smart? Me? Oh, no!" he said. "I'm not really smart. I just broke out of the strongest prison in England, that's all! And captured a train and escaped on it, that's all! And disguised myself and went around fooling everybody, that's all! Oh, no! I'm just silly old Toad! I'll tell you one or two of my little adventures, Mole, and you can judge for yourself!"

"Well, well," said Mole, "why don't you talk while I eat? I haven't had a bite since breakfast!"

"Tell us how things look at Toad Hall," Rat said quickly to Mole, "and what you think we should do, now that Toad is back."

"It's a bad situation," Mole said gloomily, "and I don't know *what* to do. Badger and I keep walking all around the house, and the weasels and stoats just laugh at us."

"Well," said Rat, "I've been thinking about it, and I think Toad should —"

"No!" cried Mole. "You're wrong! He should —"

"I won't!" shouted Toad. "It's my house, and I'll decide —"

By this time they were all talking at once.

Then Badger spoke up. "Be quiet, all of you!" They all fell silent.

"Toad!" he said severely. "You bad little animal! Aren't you ashamed of yourself?

What do you think your father, my old friend, would have said if he knew what you've been up to?"

Toad began to sob.

"There, there!" said Badger, more kindly. "Stop crying. I know you're going to try to be a better Toad from now on. But what Mole says is true. The stoats are on guard."

"Then it's all over," sobbed Toad. "I'll never see my dear Toad Hall again!"

"Cheer up, Toady!" said Badger. "I haven't said my last word yet. Now I'm going to tell you a secret."

Toad sat up and dried his eyes. He loved secrets.

"There is an underground passage," said Badger, "that leads from the river-bank right up into the middle of Toad Hall."

"Oh, come on, Badger," said Toady. "I know every inch of Toad Hall, inside and out. There's no such thing!"

"My young friend," said Badger, "your father was a friend of mine, and he told me things he wouldn't have dreamed of telling you. He discovered that passage and he thought it might come in handy someday, in case of trouble or danger, so he showed it to me. 'Don't tell my son about it,' he said. 'He's a good boy, but he can't keep a secret. If he's ever in real trouble, you may tell him.'"

Toad looked surprised. Then he smiled sheepishly. "Well, well," he said, "I guess Father was right. I do like to talk and tell secrets. Anyway, Badger, how will this passage of yours help us?"

"There's going to be a big dinner party at Toad Hall tomorrow night," Badger told them. "It's the Chief Weasel's birthday, I believe, and all the weasels will be gathered together in the dining hall, eating and drinking and laughing and carrying on."

"But the guards will be posted as usual," said Rat.

"Exactly," said Badger, "that is my point. The weasels will trust in their guards. And that is where the passage comes in. It leads right up into the pantry, next to the dining hall!"

"Aha! That squeaky board in the pantry!" said Toad. "Now I understand it!"

"We shall creep out quietly into the pantry —" cried Mole.

"— with big sticks —" shouted Rat.

"— and rush in upon them —" said Badger.

"— and whack 'em, and send them on their way!" cried Toad happily.

"Well, then," said Badger, "our plan is settled. It's getting late. We'll make the rest of our plans tomorrow morning."

The next day, Toad came down to breakfast late, just as Mole came back from a secret errand.

"I've been having such fun!" Mole told the others. "I've been teasing the stoats!"

"I hope you've been careful, Mole," said Rat.

"Oh, yes," said Mole. "I got the idea when I found that old washerwoman dress Toad came home in yesterday, hanging out to dry. I put it on and went to Toad Hall. The guards were on the lookout, of course. "Good morning, gentlemen!" I said. "Want any washing done today?"

"They looked at me and said, 'Go away, washerwoman! We don't do any washing on duty.'"

"'Or any other time?' I asked. Ha-ha-ha! Wasn't I *funny*, Toad?"

"Silly animal!" said Toad. He was jealous, to tell the truth. He wished *he'd* thought of doing that.

"The sergeant told me to run away," said Mole, "and *I* said, 'Run away? It won't be *me* running away, pretty soon!'"

"Oh, Mole! How could you?" said Rat. Badger put down his newspaper.

"I could see them looking at one another," Mole went on, "and the sergeant said to them, 'Never mind *her*, she doesn't know what she's talking about.'"

"'Oh, don't I?' said I. 'Well, let me tell you this. My daughter, she cleans for Mr. Badger, and she heard that a hundred bloodthirsty badgers are going to attack Toad Hall this very night, from the fields. Six boatloads of rats will come up the river and land in the garden, and a gang of toads will come through the orchard. You'd better get out of here while you have the chance!' Then I pretended to run away, but I came back and spied on them. They were all so nervous! They were running around and giving orders to one another and acting all confused. And I heard them saying to one another, 'That's just like the weasels. They'll be having a great time while we ferrets and stoats have to stay out here on guard and get attacked by badgers!'"

"Oh, you idiot, Mole!" cried Toad. "You've spoiled everything!"

"Mole," said Badger quietly, "I think you have more sense in your little finger than some other animals have in their whole fat bodies. You have done a great job. Good Mole! Smart Mole!"

Now Toad was wild with jealousy, especially since he couldn't understand what Mole had done that was so smart. But before he could say anything, Badger said it was time for lunch.

After they ate, Badger suggested a nap, since they were going to have a busy night, and he headed for his armchair. Rat was too nervous to sleep, so he paced around pretending to prepare for their surprise attack. Mole, maybe to make up with Toad, asked to hear all about Toad's adventures, so Toad spent a very pleasant afternoon boasting about all he'd done since he'd last seen Mole.

The Return of the Hero

Chapter Eleven

WHEN it began to get dark, the four friends all met in the parlor. Finally, they were ready to go and Badger said, "Follow me! Mole first, because I'm very pleased with him, Rat next, Toad last. And listen, Toady! Don't chatter too much, or I'll send you back!"

Toad didn't want to be left out, so he stayed quiet. Badger led them along the river, then suddenly swung himself over the edge of the bank into a hole in the riverbank. Mole and Rat followed silently, swinging themselves into the hole, but when it was Toad's turn, of course he slipped and fell into the water with a loud splash and a squeal. His friends hauled him out, but Badger was angry and told him that the next time he made a fool of himself he would definitely be left behind.

They were finally in the secret passage, and the expedition had really begun!

It was cold and dark and damp and narrow, and poor Toad began to shiver, partly from fear and partly because he was so wet. But he did his best to keep up on the long trip through the tunnel, and finally Badger said, "We should be under the dining hall by now."

Then they heard, over their heads, the sound of people shouting and cheering and stamping on the floor and hammering on tables. Toad was frightened, but Badger just said, "They certainly are having fun, those weasels!"

They went on until the noise seemed even closer. "Hurray! Hurray!" they heard, and the stamping of little feet on the floor, and the clinking of glasses as little fists pounded on the table. "What a time they're having!" said Badger. "Come on!" They hurried along the passage until it ended, and they found themselves standing under the trapdoor that led up into the pantry.

Badger said, "Now, boys, all together!" The four of them put their shoulders to the trapdoor and heaved it back. They hoisted one another into the pantry. Now there was only a door between them and the dining hall.

Then they heard a weasel making a funny speech. "I would like to say one word about our kind host, Mr. Toad. We all know Toad! *Good* Toad, *Modest* Toad, *Honest* Toad!" The rest of the weasels were laughing and laughing.

"Let me at him!" muttered Toad, grinding his teeth.

"Hold on a minute!" said Badger. "Get ready, all of you!"

"Let me sing you a little song," went on

the weasel, "all about Toad." And he began to sing a mean song.

Badger took a firm grip on the stick he carried, looked around at the others, and cried, "The time has come! Follow me!"

He threw the door open wide.

What a squealing and a squeaking and a screeching filled the air!

The terrified weasels dove under the tables and jumped out the windows! The ferrets ran for the fireplace and got jammed in the chimney! Tables and chairs were knocked over, and glass and china crashed on the floor. It was no wonder, for the four friends were a frightening sight: mighty Badger, his whiskers bristling, his great stick whistling through the air; Mole, black and serious, holding up his stick and shouting his war cry, "A mole! A mole!"; Rat, ready for a fight; Toad, swollen to twice his ordinary size, leaping into the air with toad whoops!

The whole thing ended quickly. Up and down the whole length of the hall walked the four friends, yelling and shouting and whacking with their sticks, and in five minutes the room was cleared, except for a few weasels they kept for prisoners.

Badger told Mole to go check on the guards.

Mole jumped out a window, and Badger told the other two to set a table and find some food. "We need dinner," he said. "Come on, Toad! We've got your house back for you, and you don't even offer us a sandwich." Toad wished Badger had noticed what a brave fighter he had been, but he didn't say anything. He just looked around and found some good food that hadn't been ruined in the fight.

Just as they were sitting down to eat, Mole came back. "It's all over," he reported. "From what I can tell, when the stoats heard the noise from the hall, they ran away!"

"Excellent animal!" said Badger. "Now, there's just one more thing I want you to do, Mole. I want you to take those fellows on the floor there upstairs with you and have some bedrooms cleaned out and made really comfortable. Clean sheets and all. Then you can come have supper. I'm very pleased with you, Mole!"

Mole picked up a stick, lined up his prisoners, and marched them upstairs. After a while, he came back and said that every room was ready. Then he pulled his chair up to the table to eat.

Toad put all his jealousy behind him and said, "Thank you, dear Mole, for all your trouble tonight, and especially for your cleverness this morning!" They finished their supper happily and went to bed to rest on clean sheets, glad to have won back Toad Hall.

At breakfast the next morning, Badger told Toad that he really should have a dinner party to celebrate getting his house back. In fact, Badger told Toad he should write out the invitations that very day. "Now, sit down at that table. Write invitations to all our friends, and if you stick

with it we'll get them out before lunchtime. I'll help out by ordering all the food
for the party."

"What!" cried Toad. "Stay indoors and
write a lot of stupid letters on a morning
like this? I want to go around my property
and make sure everything's all right, and
swagger about and enjoy myself! No, thank
you! I'll be — wait a minute! Why, of
course, dear Badger! It shall be done. I'll
give up this morning in honor of our
friendship."

Badger looked at Toad very suspiciously,
but Toad just smiled. And as soon as Badger left the room, Toad hurried to the
table. He had thought of a wonderful idea
while he was talking. He would write the
invitations, and he would make sure to
mention his leading part in the fight, and
he would hint at his adventures, and on
the inside of each invitation he would list
a sort of a program of entertainment for
the evening — something like this:

SPEECH . . . BY TOAD.

(There will be other speeches by Toad during the evening.)

LECTURE . . . BY TOAD.

CONTENTS: Our Prison System — The Waterways of Old England — Horse Dealing — Back to the Land — A Typical English Squire.

SONG . . . BY TOAD. (Composed by Toad himself.)

OTHER COMPOSITIONS . . . BY TOAD will be sung in the course of the evening by the . . . COMPOSER.

The idea made him very happy, and he worked very hard and got all the letters finished by noon. Just then a weasel showed up at the door, asking if there was anything he could do. Toad gave him the letters and told him to deliver them as fast as he could.

When the other animals came back for lunch after a morning on the river, Mole looked at Toad, expecting him to be mad about having to work all morning. But instead, Toad was so happy that Mole began to suspect something was up. Rat and Badger did, too.

As soon as lunch was over, Toad said he was heading off to the garden. He planned to work on some ideas for his speeches. But Rat grabbed his arm.

Toad tried to get away, but Badger grabbed his other arm, and he knew they'd caught him. The two animals took him into a small room, shut the door, and put him into a chair. Then they both stood in front of him, while Toad sat glaring back at them.

"Now, Toad," said Rat, "it's about this dinner. I'm sorry to have to speak to you like this. But we want you to understand clearly, once and for all, that there are going to be no speeches and no songs. Try to understand that we're not arguing with you, we're just telling you."

Toad saw that he was trapped. They knew him too well. His dream was over. "Couldn't I sing just one little song?" he begged.

"No, not one little song," replied Rat firmly, even though he felt terrible when he saw how disappointed Toad was. "Toady, you know your songs are all boasting. It's for your own good. You know you have to turn over a new leaf sooner or later, and this seems like a perfect time to do it."

Toad thought for a long time. Finally, he raised his head. "You have won, my friends," he said sadly. "It was a small thing that I asked, but you are right and I am wrong. From now on I will be a very different toad. Oh, what a hard world!"

And wiping tears from his eyes, he left the room.

"Badger," said Rat, "I feel terrible. What about you?"

"Oh, I know, I know," said Badger gloomily. "But it had to be done. Toad has to live here. Do you want him to be laughed at forever by the stoats and weasels?"

"Of course not," said Rat. "And speaking of weasels, it's lucky we met that little weasel just as he was leaving with Toad's invitations. I read one or two, and they were just awful. I took them all, and Mole is writing some new ones."

At last it was almost time for the dinner. Toad was in his bedroom, thinking. Soon he began to smile. Then he started giggling. Finally, he got up, locked the door, pulled the curtains across the windows, took all the chairs in the room and put them in a circle, and stood in front of them. Then he bowed, coughed twice, and began to sing. He sang the most boastful song ever, all about his heroic homecoming. He sang loudly and happily,

and when he was done he sang it all over
again.

He gave a long, long sigh.

Then he straightened his bow tie and
went downstairs to greet his guests.

All the animals cheered when he came
in, and crowded around to congratulate
him, but Toad just smiled and said, "It was

nothing. Badger was the mastermind, Mole and Rat did all the work. I just helped a little." The animals were surprised that Toad was not boasting. They gave him even more attention, and Toad discovered that he liked that.

Badger had ordered all the best food, and the dinner was a great success. There was a lot of talking and laughter, but Toad was very quiet. Some of the younger animals tried to make him sing a song or make a speech, but he wouldn't.

Toad had really changed.

From then on, the four animals led a peaceful life. Toad sent a pretty gold necklace to the warden's daughter, with a nice letter. He also thanked the train engineer and even sent some money to the bargewoman, to pay for her horse.

Sometimes, on long summer evenings, the friends would take a walk together in the Wild Wood. It was a safe place for them now. The mother weasels would tell their young ones, "Look, baby! There goes the great Mr. Toad! And that's the gallant Rat, a wonderful fighter, walking with him! And here comes the famous Mr. Mole you've heard so much about!" And when their children were having temper tantrums, their mothers would tell them that the terrible badger would get them if they didn't behave. Of course, Badger loved children, so it wasn't quite true. But it always worked.

Classic Editions of Timeless Tales...for Today's Readers

Scholastic Junior Classics